Cute Christmas!

A GOLDEN BOOK · NEW YORK

This book is based on the TV series Peppa Pig. Peppa Pig is created by Neville Astley and Mark Baker.
Peppa Pig © Astley Baker Davies Ltd/Entertainment One UK Ltd 2003.
www.peppapig.com

ISBN 978-0-593-11895-5
rhcbooks.com
PENCIL MANUFACTURED IN TAIWAN
Book printed in the United States of America
10 9 8 7 6 5 4 3 2 1

2019 Golden Books Edition

It's Christmastime!
Peppa Pig and her family are so excited!

Peppa is getting ready for Christmas.
Draw a Christmas tree on her dress.

Peppa's little brother, George, wants to join in the fun.
Draw a Santa hat on his head.

Peppa is waiting for Santa.

Peppa has a sweet surprise for you!
Connect the dots to find out what it is.

Answer on p. 127

Peppa loves to make her house look festive.

Help Peppa get ready to go outside to play in the snow.
Draw her a warm hat, a coat, and mittens.

Help George get to Peppa so they can go ice-skating.

START

FINISH

Answer on p. 127

Peppa is skating on the ice.
Draw yourself skating with Peppa!

George and Peppa love when it snows.
Draw snowflakes in the sky.

Candy Cat and Danny Dog are going skiing.

Which path does Peppa need to take to get to her friends so they can go skiing together?

Answer on p. 127

Help George find the row of snowflakes that is not like the others.

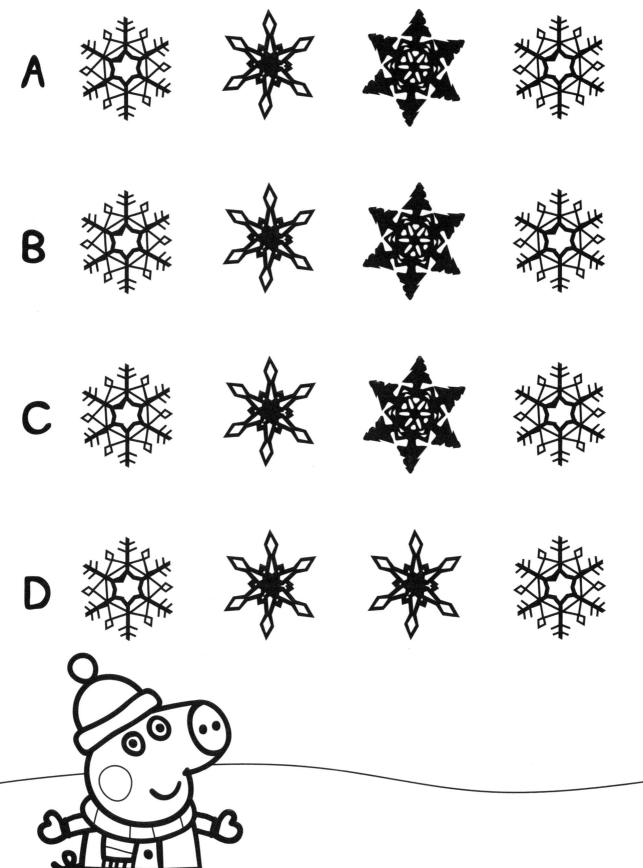

Answer on p. 127

Draw a hat, eyes, a nose, and a mouth to
complete Peppa's snowman.

One of these snowmen is not like the others.
Circle it.

Answer on p. 127

Peppa and her friends are at school making presents out of clay.

Madame Gazelle teaches Peppa and her friends
a new Christmas dance.

FA LA LA LA LA LA

Peppa and George are on Santa watch.
Draw Santa and his reindeer in the sky.

Match Peppa and her friends to their names.

Emily Elephant

Candy Cat

Peppa Pig

Rebecca Rabbit

Zoe Zebra

Answer on p. 127

Peppa and George want to draw Christmas stars.
Draw some for them.

Draw Rebecca Rabbit a snowman balloon.

Suzy Sheep and Peppa are best friends.
Can you find Suzy?

Peppa and George can't wait for Christmas!
Draw pretty patterns on the presents.

Peppa is practicing magic with Teddy for the Christmas show.
Draw Teddy popping out of the magic hat.

The Pig family is wearing matching pajamas!

George is hoping for an extra special Christmas present.

Draw a present for Peppa.

There are all kinds of good foods for Christmas.
Circle the foods you like to eat.

Daddy Pig loves eating mince pies. Yum!

Peppa and Mummy Pig want to wear matching outfits.
Draw a snowman on Mummy Pig's shirt so they match.

Granny Pig is showing Peppa how to bake Christmas cookies.

Cookie time!
Draw some Christmas cookies on Mummy Pig's tray.

It is a starry night.
How many stars can you count?

I counted _____ stars.

Answer on p. 127

Ho! Ho! Ho!
Decorate the Santa hat on Peppa.

Circle the small Santa Peppa that matches the one below.

Answer on p. 127

Peppa and her friends like to sing Christmas carols.

Peppa wants to dress Teddy up as Santa.
Draw a Santa hat on him.

Circle George's favorite toy.

Answer on p. 127

Peppa is having a tea party with Zoe, Suzy, and Rebecca.
Draw some Christmas snacks for them to eat.

The Pig family is going to get their Christmas tree.
Beep! Beep!

The Pig family is looking for the perfect Christmas tree. Circle the one that you like.

Connect the dots to see Peppa's tree.

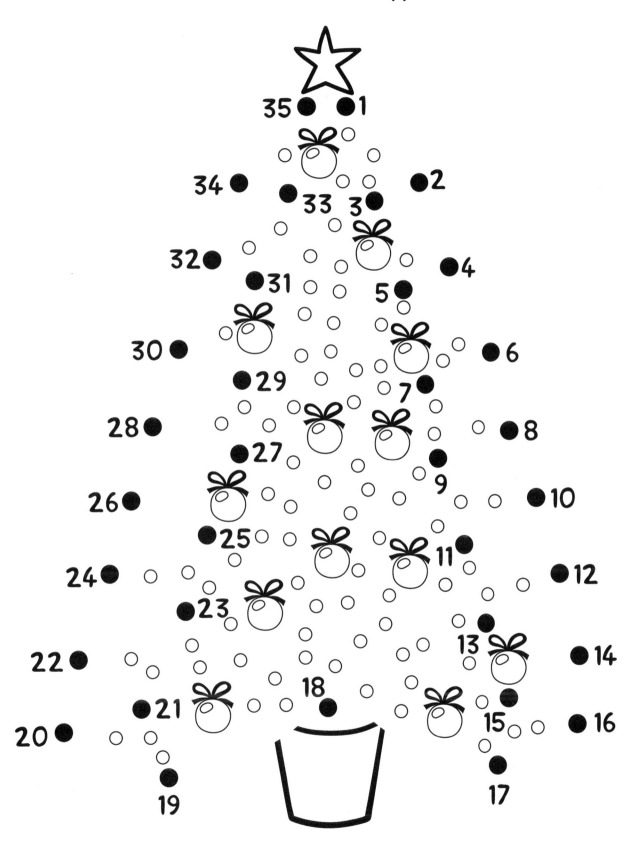

Answer on p. 127

Decorate the Christmas tree for Peppa and her family.

Peppa and George are decorating the Christmas tree.

Draw more presents under Peppa's Christmas tree.

George pretends he is looking for a yeti.
Can you find it?

Daddy Pig is having a jolly time watching
a Christmas special on TV.

George made a Christmas card for Granny Pig.

Peppa thinks she sees Santa.
Can you find Santa?

George is playing a reindeer in the school play.
Draw antlers on him.

Circle the row of holiday cards that is not like the others.

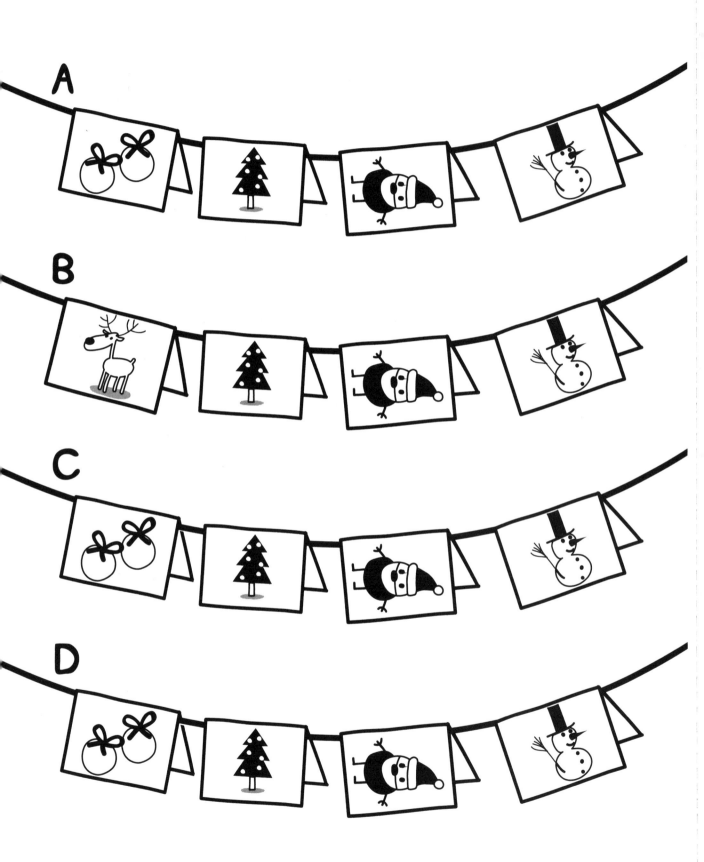

Answer on p. 127

Get Peppa to the Christmas tree so she can place a present underneath it for George.

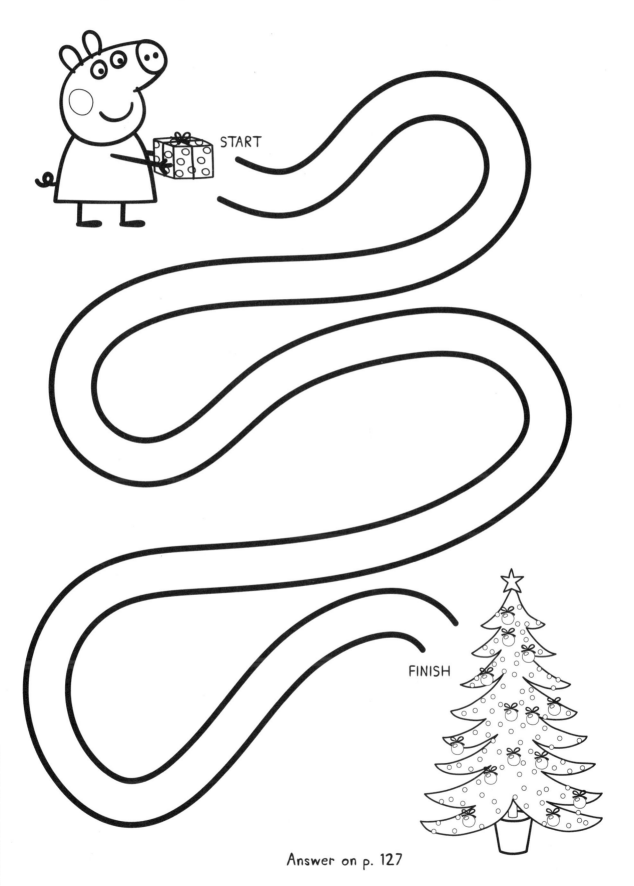

START

FINISH

Answer on p. 127

Nothing is better than a Christmas present made by someone you love.

Connect the dots to see whose big hugs keep
Peppa warm at Christmas—and all year long!

Answer on p. 127

Help Granny and Grandpa Pig get to Peppa's house so they can spend the holidays together.

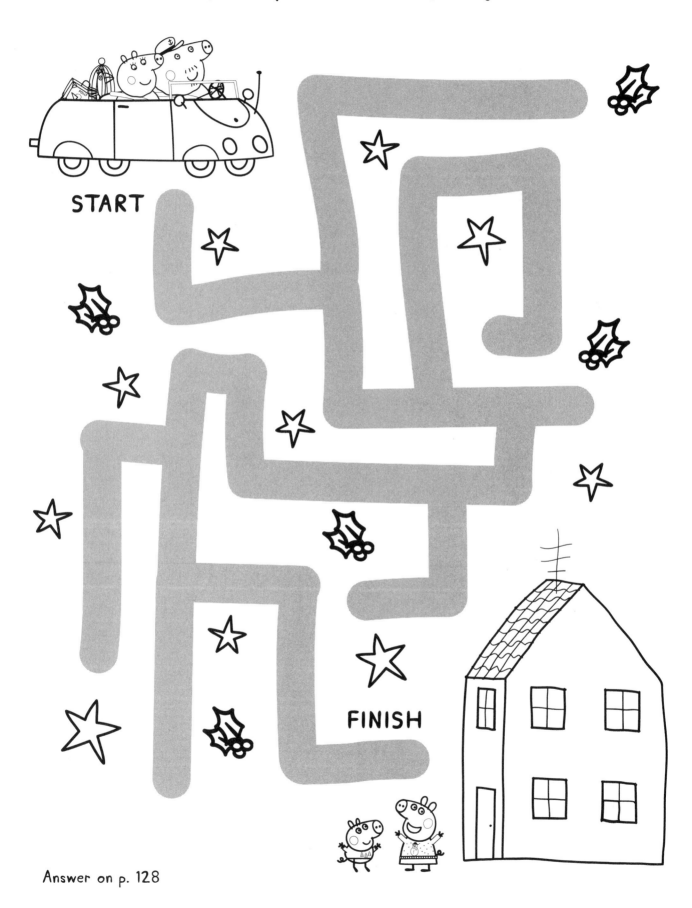

START

FINISH

Answer on p. 128

Granny Pig brings treats for the Pig family.
Circle the treats that you would like.

All aboard the Christmas train with Grandpa Pig!

George and Edmond Elephant are going
to have a snowball fight.
How many snowballs can you count?

Answer on p. 128

I counted ____ snowballs.

Peppa made Mummy Pig a pretty crown for Christmas.
Draw a crown on Peppa.

The Pig family is wearing crowns!
Circle the five differences between the top and bottom pictures.

Answer on p. 128

Draw yourself with a crown on your head.

Peppa is tickling Mummy Pig.
Mummy Pig is snorting with laughter!

George has invited Richard Rabbit to play
with his new model train.
Draw another train on the track for Richard.

Peppa loves playing music on her new guitar.

George and Peppa play beautiful music together.

Peppa's friends want to join the band.
Draw a triangle for Pedro Pony and a flute for Emily Elephant.

Daddy Pig and Peppa are buying records at the music store. Draw a record for Peppa.

Peppa dresses up and dances to a new record.

Mummy Pig and Peppa are baking a cake
for the Christmas party.
Decorate the cake to make it festive.

Granny Pig has baked a pie.
Use the code below to find out what kind of pie it is.

__ __ __ __ __

Answer on p. 128

Mummy Pig helps Peppa bake lots
of yummy treats for Christmas.
Circle your favorite treats.

George builds a snow-dino. Roar!

Peppa is wearing a colorful hat.
Color the feathers, flowers, and fruit.

Circle the hat that you will wear to the Christmas party.

Peppa and George bounce around the house.

Mummy and Daddy Pig are under the mistletoe!

Color these Christmas candies.

Zoe and Peppa are having a sleepover.

Peppa and Wendy Wolf are playing.
Draw Wendy a ball.

George has written a letter to Santa.

POST

santa
THE NORTH POLE

Write to Santa and ask him to bring a special present for your best friend.

Dear Santa,
Please bring
_____
(friend's name)

a _____
(gift)
for Christmas.
Thank you.
Love, _____
(your name)

To: Santa
The North Pole

North Pole

Peppa and Candy Cat go sledding in the snow.
Whee!

Connect the dots to see Peppa's Christmas stocking.

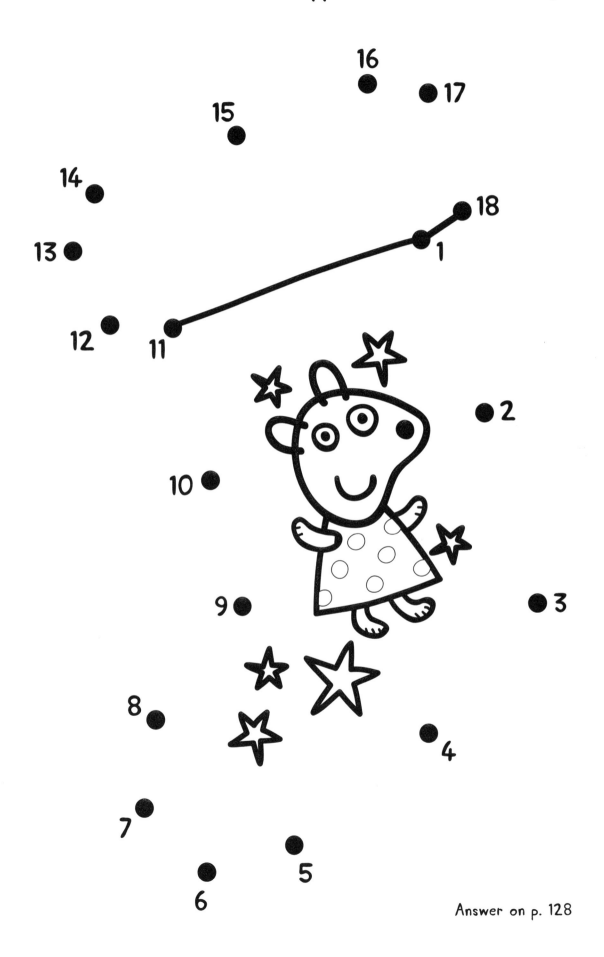

Answer on p. 128

Decorate your Christmas stocking.

Peppa loves that Christmas is on the same day in December every year. Circle that day below.

1 2 3 4 5 6

7 8 9 10 11

12 13 14 15 16

17 18 19 20 21

22 23 24 25

26 27 28

29 30 31

Answer on p. 128

Peppa and her friends practice singing Christmas carols.
Circle the row of friends that is not like the others.

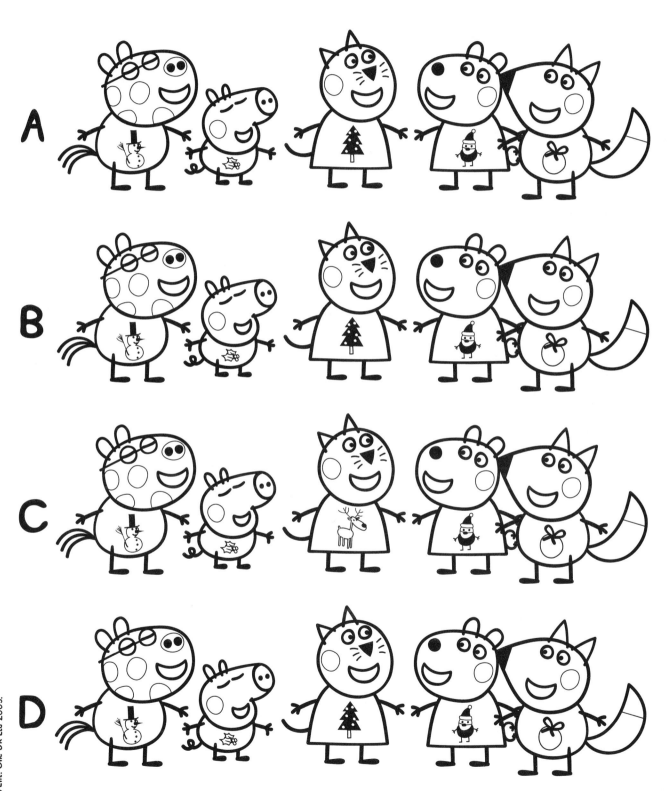

Answer on p. 128

Circle the image of Rebecca Rabbit that is different.

Answer on p. 128

Peppa plays a princess in her Christmas ballerina dance.

Peppa loves to sing. Do you want to sing along?

Suzy and Peppa give each other a hug.

Emily and Peppa like to share
their toys with each other.

Match each character to their Christmas stocking.

Answer on p. 128

It's bath time for Peppa and George.
How many towels can you count?

Answer on p. 128

I counted ____ towels.

Peppa and George brush their teeth before going to bed.
Brush! Brush! Brush!

Peppa and George put out treats for Santa.
How many can you count?

Answer on p. 128

I counted ____ treats.

Daddy Pig reads Peppa and George a Christmas story.

These piggies are tired and need to go to sleep. Yawn!

Peppa and George are cozy and warm in their pajamas.
Draw Teddy and Mr. Dinosaur so they can go to bed.

Peppa and George are all snuggled in bed.
Draw what they are dreaming about.

Santa is on his way!
Draw some more reindeer.

Hooray! It's Christmas!

George loves his new toy plane!

Peppa is teaching George some fun tricks with her new yo-yo!
Draw a yo-yo for George.

Draw what you think Peppa and George
gave Daddy Pig for Christmas.

Answer on p. 128

How many jingle bells can you count?

I counted ____ bells.

Peppa and Zoe Zebra are wearing their new dresses.
They both look very pretty.
Draw yourself in a new outfit.

Suzy Sheep has invited Peppa to see her new dollhouse.
They are playing with Teddy and Owl.

Peppa loves spaghetti, but she always makes a mess!
Tee-hee!

George has a special present for Mr. Dinosaur.
Draw a present for him.

Decorate these yummy Christmas cupcakes.

Color the portraits on the Pig family tree.

Granny and Grandpa Pig have a special gift
for George and Peppa.

Surprise! It's a jack-in-the-box!

Peppa and George are making special cookies
for Granny and Grandpa Pig.
Draw the cookies you would make.

Peppa and George like to roast marshmallows.
How many marshmallows can you count?

I counted ____ marshmallows.

Answer on p. 128

Peppa paints a picture for her best friend, Suzy Sheep.

Draw a picture of your favorite Christmas memory.

The Pig family is going to build a snowman.

Connect the dots to see the snowman.

Answer on p. 128

Circle the friend who has a different hat.

Answer on p. 128

Peppa loves to snowboard.
Decorate her snowboard.

Draw a picture of something you would like for Christmas.

Have a holly jolly Christmas!

Merry Christmas!

ANSWERS

Page 6

Page 9

Page 13

Path B

Page 14

Row D

Page 16

Page 20

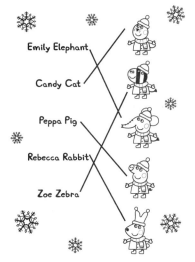

Emily Elephant

Candy Cat

Peppa Pig

Rebecca Rabbit

Zoe Zebra

Page 34

I counted 14 stars.

Page 36

Page 39

Page 43

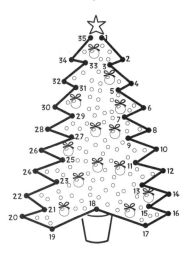

Page 52

Row B

Page 53

Page 55

ANSWERS

Page 56

Page 59

I counted 14 snowballs.

Page 61

Page 71

Apple

Page 84

Page 86

1 2 3 4 5 6
7 8 9 10 11
12 13 14 15 16
17 18 19 20 21
22 23 24 (25)
26 27 28
29 30 31

Page 87

Row C

Page 89

Page 93

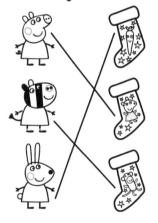

Page 94

I counted 4 towels.

Page 96

I counted 7 treats.

Page 106

Page 107

I counted 4 bells.

Page 117

I counted 7 marshmallows.

Page 121

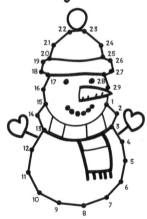

Page 122